Walt Disney
FAIRY TALE
TREASURY

Contents

Twin Books

GALLERY BOOKS
An imprint of W.H. Smith Publishers Inc.
112 Madison Avenue
New York, New York 10016

Published by Gallery Books
An Imprint of W H Smith Publishers Inc.
112 Madison Avenue
New York, New York 10016 USA

Produced by Twin Books
15 Sherwood Place
Greenwich, CT 06830 USA

ISBN 0-8317-9292-2

Printed in Hong Kong

1 2 3 4 5 6 7 8 9 10

The Pied Piper of Hamelin

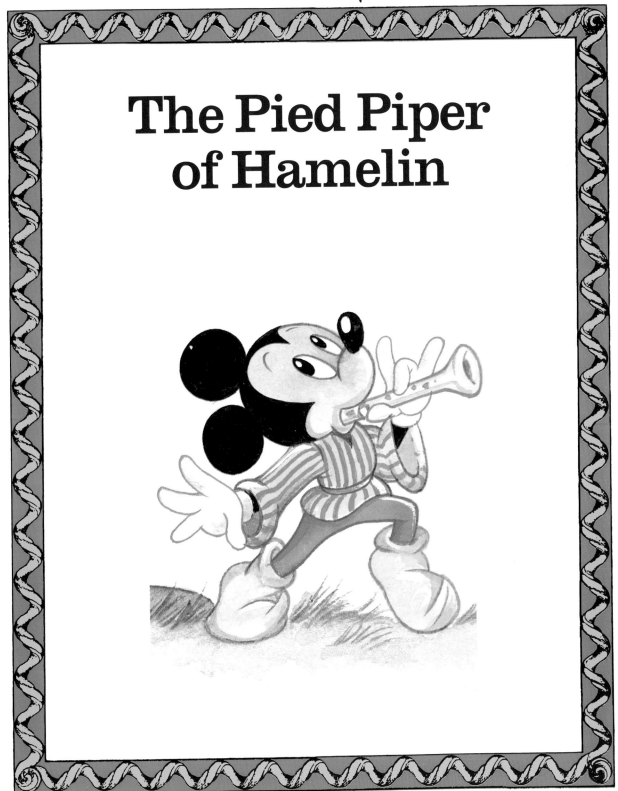

Once upon a time, there was a happy little town called Hamelin. It was set in a beautiful valley ringed by tall mountains, and was surrounded by a strong wall that protected it from attack. The only way in or out of the town was by its stout, well-guarded city gate.

The houses in Hamelin nestled together along neat cobblestone streets. All the streets led to the town square, where the town hall and the church stood.

The people who lived in this neat, well-protected town called cheerful greetings to each other as they went about their business—until the day when something happened that turned their peaceful, prosperous world upside-down.

The town was invaded! Not by hostile humans but by a horde of rats. In no time, they took over every dwelling—even the church and town hall. They crawled through the walls and over the roofs, they climbed up drainspouts and into windows, they took over houses and shops, until the poor people were afraid even to get into their own pantries and cellars!

The rats ate grain and flour, carrots and peas, roast pork and beef stew. There wasn't a kitchen free of them. There wasn't a room in the house where they couldn't be found. The rats were eating everyone out of house and home.

No one had any idea what to do about the rats, but they knew something had to be done, and fast! The mayor called a meeting at the town square.

Before this, the meetings in the town square had been full of peaceful, contented citizens. Now, the town square was crowded with desperate souls. The mayor knew that if he didn't do something, his job was on the line. So he made this announcement:

"This purse of gold goes to anyone who can rid our town of rats!"

"I'll do it," came a voice from the middle of the crowd. It belonged to a young man who was holding a flute. The little fellow didn't look very impressive, but no one else volunteered.

"Get rid of our rats, and the gold is yours," agreed the mayor.

As the crowd broke up, the fellow put the flute to his lips and began to play.

Soon the people heard a faint patter, as if tiny feet were marching toward the town square. The patter grew into steps, then into the thumping of thousands of feet, all heading for the square.

What was happening?

The rats were streaming out of the houses and shops of Hamelin, heading toward the town square, where the piper was playing his music. Slowly he turned and began to walk toward the city gates. The rats followed.

When he reached the gates, the piper turned toward the river, followed by the tramping horde. He waded into the water, still playing his flute.

The rats followed him into the water, every last one. And every last one drowned. Hamelin was saved!

The piper walked back to the city gates, expecting the townspeople to thank him for his wonderful trick. But they were all so busy celebrating that no one remembered to invite him to the party. They had even locked him out of town.

Annoyed at being left out, the piper hammered on the gates. The mayor came to see what he wanted.

"Purse of gold? What purse of gold?" the mayor blustered. "But that was a nice tune you played. Here's a coin for your trouble."

"See here, Mr. Mayor," said the piper, "you promised me a reward to get rid of the rats, and I got rid of them. I want my purse of gold, or you'll be sorry!"

Well, the mayor thought he was bluffing, and so did the townspeople. When he began to play on his flute again, they went back to their party and forgot about him.

They didn't notice when the children left the party, and when they opened the gates. They never realized that their sons and daughters were following the piper out of town, just as the rats had done!

Suddenly, the stingy mayor noticed something was wrong. He had turned to say something to his son, but found him missing. Soon all the townspeople noticed that their children were missing. They crowded toward the gates, just in time to see the last of the youngsters follow the piper away from the town.

"Wait! Wait!" yelled the frantic mayor.

"Wait! Wait!" shouted the frantic parents.

Their pleas went unnoticed. It was as if the children couldn't hear them. Off they went after the piper, singing and dancing to the music of his wonderful flute. Nothing the people of Hamelin said could call them back.

The merry band wove its way across the valley and into the foothills, joking and laughing all the way. The road became steeper, beginning its climb into the mountains. Still the children sang and danced, as if they had not a care in the world.

The townspeople watched as the children got farther and farther away.

"They're heading for the mountain trail," someone pointed out.

"They'll have to turn back there," said the mayor confidently. "That trail is too long and steep. We'll soon see them back."

But the children continued to follow the piper. At the end of the line was the mayor's son, who walked with a crutch because he had sprained his ankle playing tag. It was hard for him to keep up with the other children, but he limped along bravely, because he loved the piper's music.

The children of Hamelin were deep in the mountains when the piper finally stopped playing. In front of a wall of rock, he gathered them together and played a special short tune.

Suddenly, a gate opened in the rock, revealing a wonderful place filled with candy, fruit, and all kinds of good things to eat.

When the piper invited them to enter, the children poured through the gate, laughing with delight.

What a paradise it was! There were trees to climb, candy canes to savor, refreshing fruits to enjoy. The children of Hamelin played all day long—tag and hide-and-seek and giant-step—all the games that children everywhere love.

Not one child would ever tire of this magical land. The mountain would ring with their joyful laughter forever. They would never grow old, and never know hunger or thirst, or weariness or pain. The piper had given the children of Hamelin a wonderful gift.

19

The piper watched them, content. He'd had his revenge on the mayor and the townspeople, and the pleasure of making all these children happy, as well. He sat down under a candy tree and played another few notes on his flute. The gate in the mountain closed, shutting them all off from the world outside.

If only the piper had waited a few moments more.

The mayor's son reached the wall too late to join the other children. All he found was a jumble of rocks. He could hear the children behind it, but he couldn't find a way in. For a while he stayed up on the mountain, hoping the gate would open again. But finally, he turned and made his way down the mountain and across the valley to Hamelin.

When he got home, the mayor's son told everyone about the marvelous land in the mountains where the piper had taken the other children. The people were sad because they had lost their children even though these children would be happy in their new life. And they were sorry that they had learned an important lesson too late—a promise must always be kept.

Jack and the Beanstalk

Once upon a time, there was a place called Happy Valley. A fellow named Jack lived there, happy and carefree.

His two friends, Jim and Tom, took care of the vegetable garden, while Jack took care of the cow, whose name was Flossy.

"Give us rich milk, Flossy," said Jack, as he milked her
each day.

All of the goodness that the people of Happy Valley enjoyed
came from the castle, where a wonderful instrument lived...the
singing harp!

She was a magical living harp, as beautiful as any princess on earth. Each morning, she stood on the balcony of the castle, playing sweet, gentle music that could be heard throughout the land. All who heard the music were happy, and there was no reason to think that this happiness would ever end.

But one day a terrible noise was heard. The ground shook. The sky became dark. Terror struck the hearts of all in the valley. The little harp saw a huge hand coming toward her. She leaned back, back, back, but couldn't escape. The huge hand seized her, lifted her into the air, and stole her away.

The sweet melodies of the singing harp were no longer heard in the valley. Sadness and misfortune fell on the land. The garden that Tom and Jim had planted no longer grew, Flossy no longer gave milk, and the house where the three friends lived fell into ruin.

Together, they decided to sell the only thing of value they had left—their cow. With a heavy heart, Jack led Flossy off to market, where he would say good-bye to her for the last time.

On the way to market, Jack ran into an old man.

"Where are you going?" asked the man.

"Alas," he said, "I have to go to market and sell Flossy."

"Poor boy!" the old man exclaimed. "Are you that hungry? Then I will trade you your cow for this handful of magic beans. Plant them, and you will always have enough food to eat."

Jack was so sad that he didn't even bargain. With tears in his eyes, he handed Flossy over.

"Are you crazy?!" yelled Tom, when Jack came back with a fistful of beans. "You gave up Flossy for *those?*"

Jack tried to explain that the beans were magic, but Tom wouldn't listen. Quivering with anger, he flung the beans to the floor, and watched them disappear through a hole in the wood.

The three went to bed hungry. That night, a mysterious moon rose, and as it shone into the room, a vine pushed its way through the hole in the floor. The vine grew...and grew...and grew! One of the magic beans had taken root in the ground. It grew through the roof, then lifted the house itself toward the moon.

It was amazing! The house was perched on top of the giant beanstalk, high up in the sky! Holding onto the windowsills for dear life, Jack, Tom and Jim saw a castle, similar to the one in Happy Valley. On each side of the stairway, marble lions looked ready to gobble up any visitors.

"Let's go inside!" cried Jack, the bravest of the three.

The three friends slipped cautiously under the door. Everything inside the castle was huge—the table, the chairs, the suit of armor. They were in a giant's home!

"D-d-do you r-really want to keep going?" asked Tom. Suddenly, they heard a magical melody. It seemed to come from very far away.

"There!" whispered Jack. "It's the harp. She's locked in that box."

"Hooray!" cried Jim. "We've found our good luck!"

"Quiet!" warned Jack.

"The giant will hear you!" hissed Tom.

"Sorry," said Jim in a soft voice. "I'm just so happy to hear her again!"

"We will rescue her!" said Jack bravely.

"But how?" moaned Jim.

With Jim, who was a timid soul, and Tom, who wasn't known for his caution, this rescue wasn't going to be easy.

Suddenly, the giant appeared. He was singing loudly:

I am the giant of this land!
The kingdom fits right in my hand!
Sometimes I'm big, sometimes I'm small;
I can be any size at all!

"Ha, ha!" he laughed in a deep voice. "What should I change myself into today, to keep from scaring my sweet singing harp? A bee? A duck?"

Just then, the giant spied Jack.

"Ah-ha! What's this?" roared the giant, picking Jack up by his tail.

Jack didn't want to give the giant time to get angry. Spotting a fly swatter on the table, Jack spoke in his nicest and most flattering voice: "I'll bet you can turn yourself into any animal, right? My, that's amazing, Mr. Giant! But can you turn yourself into a fly?"

"Sure, I can," answered the giant, smugly. "I'll do it right now. Just you watch!"

But Jack was in for a surprise! Instead of becoming a tiny fly, the giant turned himself into a big pink bunny!

"What are you going to do to a big pink bunny with your pathetic little fly swatter?" the giant asked. Then he burst out with a huge belly laugh.

"You see," he said, "I know that story about the ogre that turned into a fly and got squashed like a waffle. I heard it a thousand times when I was little. But now I'm big! Very big!" Suddenly, the giant turned back into himself.

"Enough of this fooling around!" he growled. "You're so small,
you're little more than snacks. I'll save you for tomorrow, and
dunk you in my coffee. Here! Stay in this box!" And he tossed the
three friends into the box along with the harp.

The giant didn't see Jack jump to the side and hide.

"Right now, I'm going to eat my supper," he said, rubbing his
belly. "Then I'm going to bed. Sweet dreams, snacks!"

After a good meal, the giant fell asleep. Jack took advantage of this to slip into his pocket and steal the key to the box. He unlocked it and started to lower the singing harp to the floor. Tom and Jim were right behind her.

"Yeow!" cried Jim suddenly, when Tom landed on his head.

"Ssshhh!" cautioned Jack. "Don't make a sound. We don't want the giant to wake up!"

The singing harp was left hanging nervously in mid-air. Jack lowered his friends quickly—too quickly, in fact. The singing harp dropped to the floor.

Boiiinnnng! went the harp.

The sound echoed through the castle.

The giant woke up and jumped to his feet. He rubbed his eyes and saw the three friends running away at full speed, carrying the harp.

"Stop!" the giant cried after them.

The three friends just kept on going. They ran through the stone-paved halls of the castle, squeezed under the huge door, then tumbled down the castle steps. They had no intention of being dunked into a steaming cup of coffee and eaten by a giant!

The trip down the magic beanstalk was like a long sled ride. Down, down they slid, along the winding, slippery stalk, until a heavy weight above them made the beanstalk start to shake.

The giant had started down the beanstalk, gasping and wheezing with every movement.

"Thieves!" he roared. "Wait until I get my hands on you!"

But as soon as Tom and Jim were safely on the ground, they began cutting down the vine.

"Faster! Faster!" begged the singing harp. "I see him coming!"

Soon the beanstalk began to sway. Then, with a loud *crack!*, it crashed to the ground.

Since the giant was so big and heavy, he landed with a loud *thud!* His fall made such a deep hole that Jack and his friends couldn't even see him anymore.

"Hurray!" they all cried. "We're free of the giant forever!"

The singing harp was returned to her place of honor in the castle, and she went to work immediately. As her beautiful melodies filled the valley, people became happy again. Crops began to grow, and cows gave milk. Once more it was a place that could rightly be called Happy Valley.

And the magic beanstalk? At the top of the vine were some more beans. Jack put them in a little box that he guarded carefully, just in case another giant should come down from the sky. He wanted to be sure that hope and prosperity would live forever in Happy Valley.

The Seven-League Boots

Once upon a time, there was a poor woodcutter and his wife who had seven sons. One day, what little food they had ran out, and they were faced with a terrible decision. "We can no longer feed our children," the woodcutter said to his wife. "The only thing we can do is to leave them deep in the forest. They'll be better off on their own."

His wife was filled with sadness. "Our poor boys! The wolves will eat them!" she cried. But she knew there was no other way. At least in the forest they would have a chance to find food.

What neither the woodcutter nor his wife knew was that their youngest son, Hop-o'-My-Thumb, had overheard their plan.

Though Hop-o'-My-Thumb was the youngest child, he was also the smartest. He went to the stream and collected a pocketful of white pebbles. Later, when his parents took everyone into the forest, Hop-o'-My-Thumb dropped the pebbles along the path.

As the boys chopped wood, their parents crept away, weeping.

When they realized their parents had left them, the brothers were afraid. "We're lost!" they cried.

All but Hop-o'-My-Thumb. "No we're not," he told them. "All we have to do is follow the pebbles that I left along the way."

Following that trail, the boys were soon home. The woodcutter and his wife were overjoyed to see their children. They had managed to sell some of the wood they had cut, and now had enough money to feed their sons—but not for long.

Soon the wretched parents were forced to abandon their children in the forest again. On this trip, Hop-o'-My-Thumb scattered a trail of bread crumbs along the path, not realizing that the birds would make a meal of them.

That night Hop-o'-My-Thumb climbed a tree. Looking into the distance, he called to his brothers, "I see a house! We're saved!"

The brothers trooped up to the door, where they were greeted by a woman. "You may come in if you wish," she told them, "but beware: The ogre who lives here eats children. If he finds you, he will certainly gobble you up!"

"Maybe he won't be hungry," said Hop-o'-My-Thumb. "Besides, if we stay out there in the forest, the wolves will surely eat us."

So the woman brought them inside and fed them a delicious supper.

They had just begun to eat when they heard a great rumbling
sound. The ogre was coming home! Quickly, the woman showed
the boys where to hide.

The ogre looked at the meal being served, then sniffed the air.
"I smell something, old woman! I smell children!"

Within moments, he had found Hop-o'-My-Thumb and his brothers. "Put away that food!" he told the woman. "I'll have these tasty little ones for dinner, instead."

"Wait until tomorrow," she suggested. "They'll be even tastier after a hot meal and a good night's sleep." Reluctantly, the ogre agreed.

The woman took the children to a bedroom that contained two huge beds. In one, the ogre's seven daughters were sleeping soundly, each with a golden crown on her head.

Hop-o'-My-Thumb and his six brothers were wearing little woolen caps, and this gave Hop-o'-My-Thumb an idea. After his brothers were asleep, he got up and went over to the girls' bed.

Hop-o'-My-Thumb swapped the woolen caps for the crowns and went back to bed.

When the ogre came upstairs to check on his next day's meal, he picked up the children with the caps and threw them into a closet for safekeeping. He didn't know he had locked up his own daughters!

After the ogre had gone, Hop-o'-My-Thumb and his brothers climbed out the window and escaped into the night.

The next morning the ogre realized what had happened and flew into a rage. "Trick me, will they?' he snarled. "Well, they won't get away with it!"

"Woman, bring me my boots—my seven-league boots! I'll catch those rascals and bring them back for my supper!"

The ogre pulled on his seven-league boots and ran out the door.

Meanwhile, Hop-o'-My-Thumb and his brothers had nearly made it to their parents' house. But the ogre was coming after them in huge strides and would catch up any second.

"Quick, let's hide under a rock," said Hop-o'-My-Thumb.

The ogre stopped to catch his breath. "Where can those rascals be?" he gasped.

"I'll just rest a moment under this tree," the ogre said to himself. "Then I'll have plenty of energy to catch those little villains!" And he fell sound asleep.

As soon as Hop-o'-My-Thumb heard the ogre begin to snore, he got another idea. On tiptoe, he sneaked up and slipped the huge boots off, very, very carefully. Then he put them on his own feet. The ogre's seven-league boots magically shrank to fit him!

Now that he was wearing the ogre's seven-league boots, Hop-o'-My-Thumb could travel twenty-one miles with every stride! This gave the clever boy yet another idea. "You go on home," he told his astonished brothers. "I have business to conduct with the king."

As his brothers set off happily for their parents' cottage, Hop-o'-My-Thumb reached the royal court in just three strides. At the castle gates, he asked to be brought before the king himself.

That very day, the king's army was busy fighting a battle a hundred leagues away. Hop-o'-My-Thumb knew that the king had heard no news and was anxious to know if his troops had won.

"Your Majesty," he said to the king, "I can bring you news of your army before the sun sets!"

"If you succeed, I'll make you rich before the sun rises again," replied the king, knowing that such a thing was impossible.

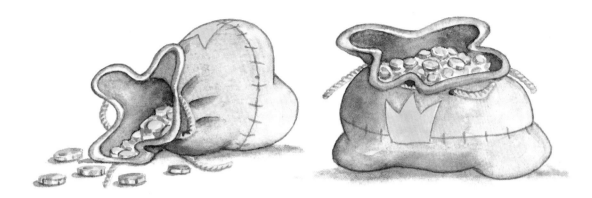

As he had promised, Hop-o'-My-Thumb brought news to the king before day's end: The royal troops had been victorious!

The grateful king kept his word and gave Hop-o'-My-Thumb a sack full of gold—and a job. He would be the king's Royal Messenger and carry orders to the captains on the battlefield.

Hop-o'-My-Thumb sent the gold home to his parents, and went to work for the king until peace returned to the kingdom. When it did, he strode home in his seven-league boots, carrying his royal salary in a huge sack upon his back.

"I'm home!" cried Hop-o'-My-Thumb when he arrived.

Joyfully his mother swept him up and gave him a big hug. Now the woodcutter's family was together once more—never again to be separated by poverty.

And so, even though Hop-o'-My-Thumb was the youngest and
smallest child of the woodcutter and his wife, he was the one who
saved the whole family with his clever ideas—and a little help
from the ogre's seven-league boots.

Hansel and Gretel

Once upon a time, there was a poor woman who lived in the forest with her husband and two children. Her husband had gone far away to find work many weeks before, and she waited anxiously to hear from him.

One day she realized that the food was almost gone. All she had left was a pot of thin soup made of dandelion leaves and spices.

"What shall I do?" cried the woman, thinking of her two hungry children. "What will become of us?"

Moments later, the miller knocked at the door. "I've brought you some flour sent by your husband," said the miller. "Perhaps you can bake cookies and sell them in town."

"What luck!" the woman said excitedly.

She quickly whipped up some cookies.

She took the first batch to town, leaving Hansel and Gretel to watch the second batch as it cooled.

"Be good while I'm away," she told the children.

The children were very excited, because their mother had given each of them a cookie. After eating hers, Gretel yawned.

"I think I'll take a nap now," she said, lying down.

"Me, too," said Hansel, closing his eyes.

While they slept, Martin, their donkey, sneaked into the house. He sniffed the cookies and bit into each of them, one by one. Then he knocked over the bag of flour. When Hansel woke up and saw what had happened, he knew that his mother would be furious.

He was right. When their mother came home and saw her kitchen, she was angrier than they had ever seen her.

"Is this how you take care of the house while I am gone?" cried their mother. "My cookies are half eaten, the flour is all over the floor, and I have nothing left to sell in town. Now how will we live?"

Hansel and Gretel hung their heads in shame. So did Martin the donkey.

"Out of the house with you!" ordered their mother. "I don't think I ever want to see you again!"

So the children went off into the forest, sure that their mother would never forgive them.

"What'll we do, Hansel?" Gretel asked.

"I know!" said Hansel, brightening. "Let's look for berries. Mother can make jam with them and sell the jars in town!"

"Where will we find these berries?" asked Gretel. But Hansel wasn't listening. A wonderful smell was tickling his nose, making him forget all about berries.

"Where are you going?" asked Gretel.

"Something smells delicious!" said Hansel, jumping over a fence along the path. "Come on! There's a chimney behind those trees. I think the smell must be coming from there."

"But Hansel, look at that sign!" Gretel pointed nervously to a sign painted with a skull and crossbones that stood in their path. "I think it means danger!"

"Aw, come on, scaredy-cat!" said Hansel, laughing.

When Hansel and Gretel reached the house nestled among the trees, they thought they had stepped into a dream. It was made of gingerbread and peppermint, of licorice and chocolate and every kind of candy imaginable.

"You see?" cried Hansel with delight. "It's a good thing you followed me! We're going to have a feast."

An old woman stepped out to greet them.

"Come in, darlings," she said in a gentle voice. "Don't be afraid. You may have anything you want. The windows are made of candy and spun sugar, the chimney is made of chocolate. There are candy canes along the window frame, giant strawberries in the garden, and the roof is made of sugar cookies—you may eat them all, if you like."

The children loved sweets, and all they could think about was stuffing themselves with the cakes, candies, and cookies she gave them.

Poor Hansel and Gretel didn't know it, but the sweet, smiling old woman was a witch.

That night, when she saw the children's eyelids begin to droop, the witch fed them another cake, frosted with sleeping potion. "Just have a little before you go to bed," she offered. "You'll sleep better."

The children slept very soundly, and didn't even wake when the witch came and took Hansel out of bed and locked him in a cage. The witch licked her lips and rubbed her greedy hands together.

"The little boy is the fattest. I'll eat him first!" she decided.

The next day, Gretel was shaken awake by the witch. "Get to work, you lazy girl!" she ordered.

What's going on? Gretel wondered.

When she saw Hansel in a cage and realized that they were prisoners, Gretel began to cry.

"Get to work!" hissed the awful witch. "You don't think you can just lie around the house all day and eat, do you?"

"Wash the dishes!" ordered the witch. "Scrub the floors! Clean the whole house—and not a morsel of food for you! I'm the only one who's going to eat today."

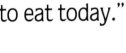

Gretel set about cleaning the house while the witch disappeared down into the kitchen.

It wasn't long before Gretel noticed a strange odor coming up from below.

Opening the door a crack, she saw a horrible sight!
Surrounded by spider webs, skulls, lizards, and all sorts of terrible objects, the witch stood before a giant cauldron, stirring a foul-smelling soup.

With an evil cackle, the witch dipped her spoon into the pot. "Mmm," she murmured, "just a bit more toad's juice, and it will be perfect. Time to put Hansel in to simmer. With all the cookies he ate, I won't need to add any sugar. Glutton stew, what a treat!"

Oh, no! thought Gretel. *She's going to eat my brother!*

Gretel crept down the staircase. Quiet as a mouse, she sneaked up behind the witch and shoved her into the soup.

"No!" cried the witch, but the soup ladle thumped her on the head and the horrible woman sank to the bottom of the pot.

Gretel quickly found the key to the cage where Hansel slept. She ran back upstairs.

"Wake up!" she cried, unlocking the cage door.

"Huh?" Hansel mumbled, rubbing his eyes. "What's up?"

"That witch was no nice old lady," Gretel told him. "She was really fattening us both up, and today she was going to have you for dinner! But I fixed her—I dumped her into her own soup."

Hansel was impressed. "Good work, sister," he said, giving her a big hug.

Since the witch could no longer harm them, the children decided to search the house. Every witch they'd ever heard about had treasure hidden somewhere. So they looked under the mattresses, in the cupboards, and all through the closets.

Everywhere they looked, they found gold.

"We're rich!" crowed Hansel.

"Wait until Mother sees this treasure!" cried Gretel. "Surely now she'll forgive us for letting Martin wreck the kitchen."

The children met their mother on the way home. "Oh, my darlings," she said, hugging them both, "I'm so sorry I was angry!"

When the children showed her the gold, she cried. "Now your father will never have to go far away to find work again!"

To celebrate their good fortune, Hansel and Gretel's mother offered to bake a cake. "No! No!" cried Hansel. "Sweets are wonderful, but we've had more than enough for a while!"